COME BACK SOON

COME

BACK SOON

Daniel Schallau

Houghton Mifflin Books for Children

Houghton Mifflin Harcourt · Boston New York 2009

For my family

Houghton Mifflin Books for Children is an imprint of
Houghton Mifflin Harcourt Publishing Company.

www.hmhbooks.com

The text of this book is set in Cronos Pro Semibold.
The art was created using colored pencils and pen and ink on watercolor paper.
Book design by Carol Goldenberg

Library of Congress Cataloging-in-Publication Data
Schallau, Daniel Page, 1966–
Come back soon / written and illustrated by Daniel Schallau.
p. cm.
Summary: A clumsy but helpful elephant makes a big impression
when he accepts an invitation from the penguins to visit Icetown.
ISBN 978-0-618-69494-5
[1. Elephants—Fiction. 2. Penguins—Fiction.] I. Title.
PZ7.S33365Co 2009
[E]—dc22
2008040459

Printed in Singapore
TWP 10 9 8 7 6 5 4 3 2 1

Every day from Icetown, hundreds of fish letters are delivered far and wide around the world.

Postwhales deliver most of the long-distance letters,
and penguins do all the rest.

From whale to ship to truck, a letter finally reaches Elephant Island.

"Ah, the mail's here," says Elephant.

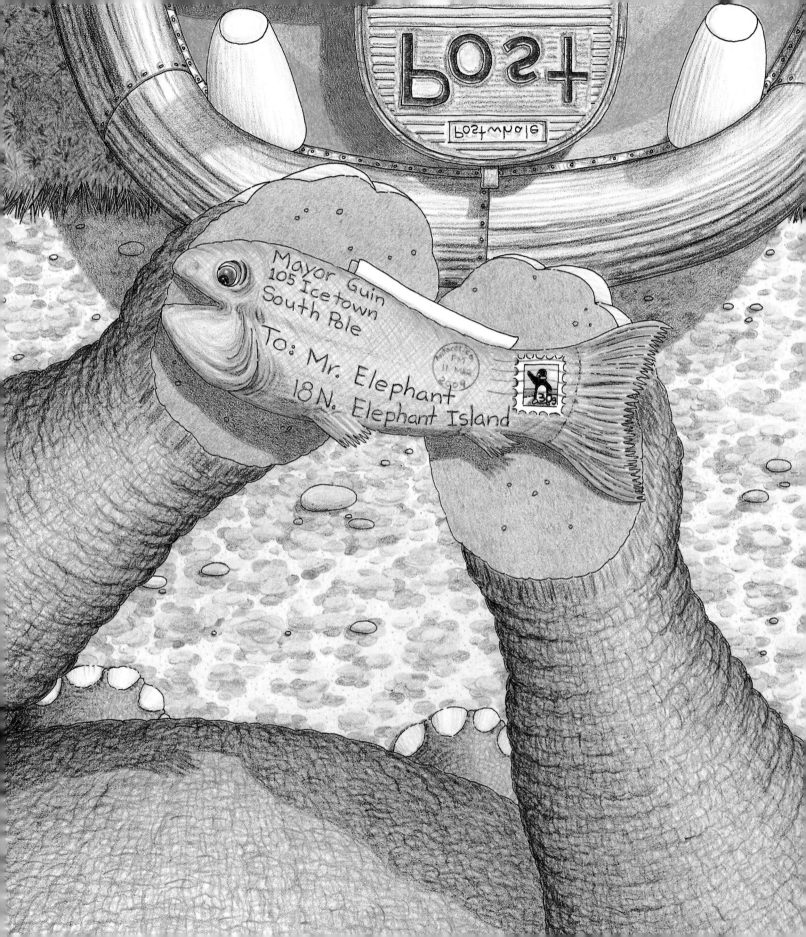

"What a nice invitation—and the envelope is delicious!"

After a tasty lunch, Elephant packs his toothbrush, toothpaste,
a towel, and scarves for everyone.

"I have the feeling I've forgotten something," Elephant worries.
"But I mustn't be late."

After many days . . .

"Ice ho!"

Meanwhile, in Icetown, the penguins wait patiently for their guest.

When Elephant arrives, his friends rush to greet him at the foot of
Hotel Penguin. Elephant helped them build it just a few months ago.

"Ahoy there! May I climb up?" Elephant asks.

After his long journey, Elephant is famished, so they roll downtown
to find a restaurant.

"Hmmm. Make that twenty-seven more bowls, please," Elephant orders.

"I knew I forgot something—my suit!" he cries.

"Is this enough?" Elephant asks. Tailor Guin tells him that his suit will be ready first thing in the morning.

Then it's back to the Hotel Penguin.

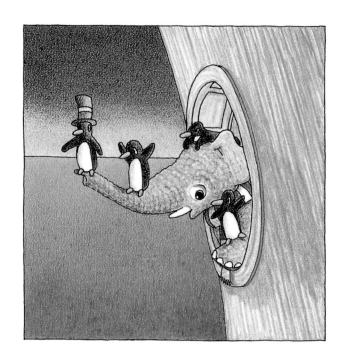

Elephant loves the view.
"Just like home," he says.

"That reminds me—
I have presents!"

When everyone is cozy in a scarf, it's time for bed.

Early the next morning, Elephant yawns. "Wake up, penguins.
It's beautiful outside."

Everyone washes his face,   **brushes his tusks or beak,**

and gets ready for the day ahead.

Breakfast is scrumptious. "I think we have time for one more pancake," says Elephant.

But suddenly he remembers. "My suit!" **CRASH!**

"We mustn't be late!" Elephant cries.

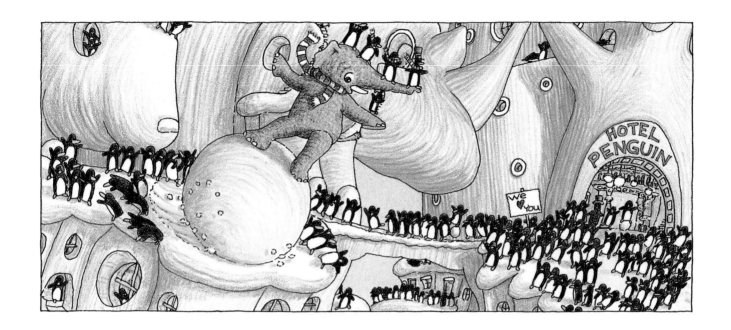

"Hold on!"

Elephant somehow manages to steer his way to Tailor Guin's.

SWOOOSH! "The suit fits perfectly—thank yooooou!"

"UH-OH!"

"Look out beloooow!"

CRACK!

SPLOOOSH!

"Is everyone all right?" Elephant asks.

After they float at sea for many hours, Mayor Guin finally arrives with Bernie the postwhale.

When Icetown is close, some penguins swim home, while others keep Elephant company.

Back on ice, they immediately begin rebuilding. "This is a job
for an elephant!"

Forty-eight loads of snow later, the hotel begins
to take shape.

In less than a week, it's finished.

Finally, the dedication.

After the ceremony, everyone glides down to the foot of the giant penguin to say goodbye.

"I had so much fun . . . but I caused so much trouble. I'm sorry,"
Elephant sighs.

The penguins quickly make a
snowball: *pat, pat, pat.*

Dive, dive, dive.

Swim, swim, swim.

"Is this for me?" Elephant asks.